LITTLE HOUSE
Laura Ingalls Wilder

MY FIRST LITTLE HOUSE BOOKS

CHRISTMAS IN THE BIG WOODS

ADAPTED FROM THE LITTLE HOUSE BOOKS

By Laura Ingalls Wilder

Illustrated by Renée Graef

HARPERCOLLINS PUBLISHERS

For my dad
—R.G.

Christmas in the Big Woods Text adapted from Little House in the Big Woods, *text copyright 1932, copyright renewed*
1959, Roger Lea MacBride. Illustrations © 1995 by Renée Graef. *Printed in the U.S.A.* All rights reserved.
Library of Congress cataloging-in-Publication Data Wilder, Laura Ingalls, 1867–1957. *Christmas in the Big Woods / adapted from*
the little house books by Laura Ingalls Wilder ; illustrated by Renée Graef. p. cm. — (My first little house books)
Summary: A young pioneer girl and her family celebrate Christmas in their cabin in the Wisconsin woods. ISBN 0-06-024752-5. —
ISBN 0-06-024753-3 (lib. bdg.). — ISBN 0-06-443487-7 (pbk.) [1. Christmas—Fiction. 2. Frontier and pioneer life—Wisconsin—
Fiction. 3. Family life—Wisconsin—Fiction 4. Wisconsin—Fiction] I. Graef, Renée, ill. II. Series.
PZ7.W6461Ch 1995 [E]—dc20 94-14478 CIP AC
HarperCollins®, ■®, Harper Trophy®, and Little House® are registered trademarks of HarperCollins Publishers Inc.

Illustrations for the My First Little House Books are inspired by the work of Garth Williams with his permission, which we gratefully acknowledge.

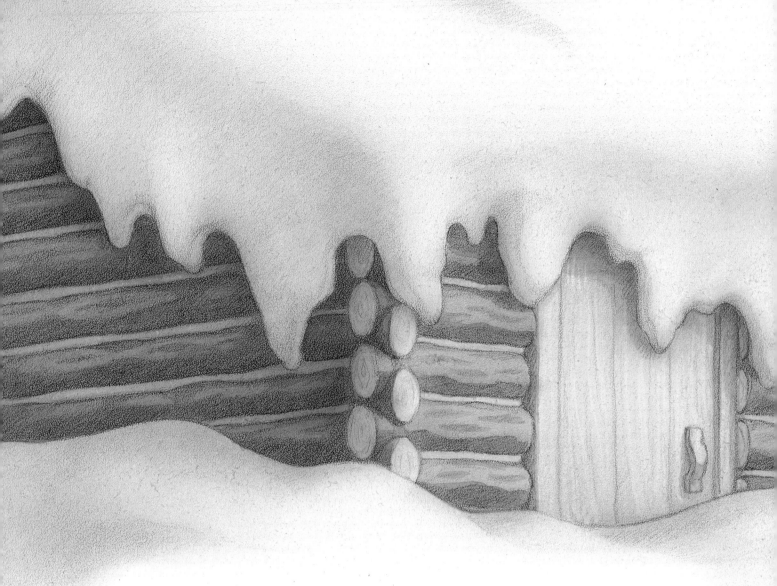

Once upon a time, a little girl named Laura
lived in the Big Woods of Wisconsin in a little
house made of logs.

Laura lived in the little house with her Pa, her Ma, her big sister Mary, her little sister Carrie, and their good old bulldog Jack.

Christmas was coming, and the little house
was covered with snow. When Pa came in from
shoveling, he caught Laura up in a big bear hug
against his cold winter coat. His mustache was
covered with melting snowflakes.

Ma was busy all day long cooking good things for Christmas. She baked bread and apple pies, and filled a big jar with cookies. Laura and Mary got to lick the spoon.

Pa and Ma showed Laura and Mary how to make molasses candy by pouring hot sugar-and-molasses syrup into pans of snow. The syrup hardened at once and turned into candy! Laura and Mary could eat one piece each, but the rest was saved for Christmas Day.

The day before Christmas, Aunt Eliza, Uncle Peter, and cousins Peter, Alice, and Ella came to visit. Laura and Mary heard sleigh bells ringing, and then a big bobsled came out of the woods. Aunt Eliza, Uncle Peter, and the cousins were inside covered up with blankets.

When everyone came inside, the little house was filled to the seams. Jack ran around in circles, barking happily. Now there were lots of children to play with!

Laura and Mary and the cousins put on their warm coats and mittens and scarves and went outside to make pictures in the soft, deep snow.

They played so hard that when night came, they were too excited to sleep. But they knew they must, or Santa Claus would not come. So they hung their stockings by the fireplace, put on their red flannel nightgowns, and went to bed.

In the morning they all woke up almost at the same moment and ran to see what was in their stockings. In every stocking was a pair of bright red mittens and a stick of red-and-white-striped peppermint candy. They were so happy they could hardly speak.

But Laura was the happiest of all. In her stocking
was a beautiful rag doll with black button eyes
and a pink-and-blue calico dress. Laura named her
doll Charlotte, and she let all the other children
hold her.

For Christmas breakfast Ma made each child a pancake man. All the children held their plates next to the stove and watched while Ma made the pancake men one by one out of pancake batter. Peter ate his up right away, but the girls ate theirs slowly to make them last.

It was too cold to go outside, so the children played quietly inside. They ate their candy, admired their mittens, and looked at the pictures in Pa's big green book until it was time for the cousins to go home. Laura held Charlotte in her arms the whole time.

At last Aunt Eliza, Uncle Peter, and the cousins bundled up in their coats and blankets and got into the bobsled. "Good-by!" they called, and off they went into the woods. In a little while the happy sound of sleigh bells was gone, and Christmas was over. But what a happy Christmas it had been!